Giraffe
and
Bird

Rebecca Bender

pajama press

This edition first published in Canada and the United States in 2019
First published in Canada in 2017
First published in the United States in 2017 titled *Not Friends*

www.pajamapress.ca   info@pajamapress.ca

 Canada Council   Conseil des arts   ONTARIO ARTS COUNCIL
for the Arts   du Canada   CONSEIL DES ARTS DE L'ONTARIO
                                          an Ontario government agency
                                          un organisme du gouvernement de l'Ontario

The publisher gratefully acknowledges the support of the Canada Council for the Arts and the Ontario Arts Council for its publishing program. We acknowledge the financial support of the Government of Canada through the Canada Book Fund (CBF) for our publishing activities.

Library and Archives Canada Cataloguing in Publication
Title: Giraffe and Bird / Rebecca Bender.
Names: Bender, Rebecca, 1980- author, illustrator.
Description: Originally published: Toronto : Dancing Cat Books, ©2010.
Identifiers: Canadiana 20190166355 | ISBN 9781772781052 (hardcover)
Classification: LCC PS8603.E5562 G57 2019 | DDC jC813/.6—dc23

Publisher Cataloging-in-Publication Data (U.S.)
Names: Bender, Rebecca, 1980-, author, illustrator.
Title: Giraffe and Bird / Rebecca Bender.
Description: Toronto, Ontario Canada : Pajama Press, 2019. | Reprint. | Previously published in the U.S. as "Not Friends", 2017. | Summary: "Giraffe and Bird are not friends. After all, they bicker all the time. But when they go their separate ways and a scary storm strikes, they both realize they might be better off together—even if they are still not friends" -- Provided by publisher.
Identifiers: ISBN 978-1-77278-105-2 (hardcover)
Subjects: LCSH: Giraffe – Juvenile fiction. | Birds – Juvenile fiction. | Friendship – Juvenile fiction. | BISAC: JUVENILE FICTION / Social Themes / Friendship.
Classification: LCC PZ7.B464Gir |DDC [E] – dc23
Original art created with acrylic paint on texturized illustration board

Cover and book design—Rebecca Bender

Manufactured by Qualibre Inc. / Print Plus
Printed in China

Pajama Press Inc.
181 Carlaw Ave. Suite 251 Toronto, Ontario Canada, M4M 2S1
Distributed in Canada by UTP Distribution
5201 Dufferin Street Toronto, Ontario Canada, M3H 5T8
Distributed in the U.S. by Ingram Publisher Services
1 Ingram Blvd. La Vergne, TN 37086, USA

Original art created with
acrylic paint on texturized
illustration board.

For all the little birds in my life

It's true that **getting along** can be difficult.
If the bird could tell you, he'd say
he **can't stand** the giraffe.

And if the giraffe could tell you, he'd say
he can't abide the bird.

The bird, you see, makes funny faces at the giraffe.

THPLLLLBBBS!

And the giraffe sticks out
his **long tongue**
at the bird.

This makes the bird **twitter** in the giraffe's ear.

Tweet!

Tweet!
Tweet!

That makes the giraffe **invade** the bird's personal space.

Some days the giraffe has **bad breath**.

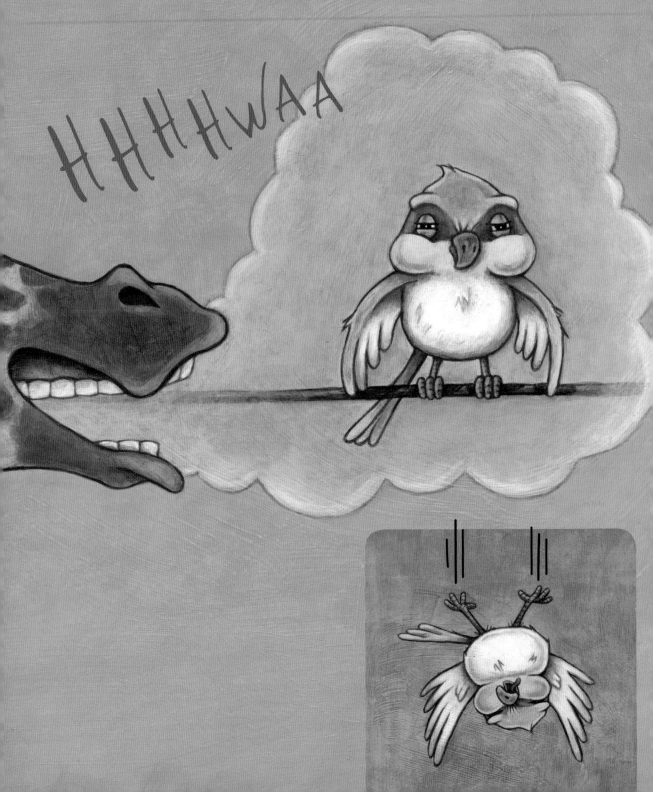

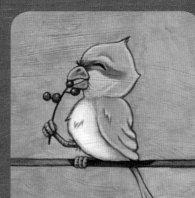

Other days the bird eats
too many berries
(which are high in fiber).

Frequently the giraffe makes loud noises when he **chews** his food with his mouth open.

Often the bird **slurps** up a **slimy worm** in front of the giraffe.

SLLLRRP

Sometimes the bird **plucks** his feathers just above the giraffe's head.

sniffle

sniffle

This makes the giraffe sneeze.

Every time the giraffe lets out a sneeze,
the bird is **blown right off**
the telephone wire.

AAACHHEEWW

W! Flap

Flap

Flap

And every time the bird is blown off the telephone wire, he flies up to **perch right on** the giraffe's horns.

When the bird perches on the giraffe's horns,
the giraffe **swats** him with his ears.

When the giraffe swats the bird with his ears,
the bird **pecks** him with his beak.

The pecking makes the giraffe shake his head until they are **both dizzy.**

Dizzy and woozy, they **both tumble** to the ground.

One day, the giraffe loses his patience and shouts at the bird,

Scram, Bird!

The bird gets fed up and shouts back at the giraffe,

Get lost, Giraffe!

So they do.

That night, there is a seriously scary storm.
All the telephone poles crash to the ground.

The giraffe wishes he could hide his eyes under
the bird's feathers so he wouldn't see the lightning.
The bird wishes he could hide under
the giraffe's ears so he wouldn't hear the thunder.

CRACK!

BOOM!

The next morning, the bird feels glum. He has nowhere to sit, and no one to pick and peck.

The giraffe feels lonely. There is
no one around
to pester and perturb him.

With no one around to pester him,
the giraffe has time to think.
The funny thing is that all the giraffe
can think about is the bird.

What can he do
to bring the bird back?

The giraffe agrees to help
the **telephone company** for a while.

He doesn't have to wait long for the bird to return.
He also doesn't have to wait long for the bird to
start **making faces again.**

Now it's true that getting along can be difficult.
And if you asked these two, the giraffe might still say
he **can't abide** the bird,

and the bird might still say
he **can't stand** the giraffe.

But we know better.

Rebecca Bender is a well-loved author-illustrator of children's books as well as an art director and designer. Her books include *Don't Laugh at Giraffe*, *Giraffe Meets Bird*, *Peach Girl* (illustration), and *How Do You Feel?*. Her awards and honors include the OLA Blue Spruce Award, a Cooperative Children's Book Center best-of-the-year choice, and a Toronto Public Library best-of-the-year selection. Rebecca graduated from the Ontario College of Art and Design at the top of her class, earning the Medal for Illustration. Rebecca lives in Burlington, Ontario, with her husband and two children. With several birds in her life, Rebecca knows how it feels to be the giraffe, and she wouldn't trade these friendships for anything.